W9-BVB-201

OIL CITY LIBRARY
2 CENTRAL AVE.
OIL CITY, PA 16301

DISCARDED

Crocs!

By David T. Greenberg

Illustrated by Lynn Munsinger

LB 1837

LITTLE, BROWN AND COMPANY
New York Boston

OIL CITY LIBRARY
2 CENTRAL AVE.
OIL CITY, PA 16301
DISCARDED

To Josiah: Coolest croc in the clan!

With admiration and love,
Duv

Copyright © 2008 by David T. Greenberg
Illustrations copyright © 2008 by Lynn Munsinger

All rights reserved. Except as permitted under the U.S. Copyright Act of 1976, no part of this publication may be reproduced, distributed, or transmitted in any form or by any means, or stored in a database or retrieval system, without the prior written permission of the publisher.

Little, Brown and Company

Hachette Book Group USA
237 Park Avenue, New York, NY 10017
Visit our Web site at www.lb-kids.com

First Edition: May 2008

Library of Congress Cataloging-in-Publication Data

Greenberg, David (David T.)
Crocs! / by David T. Greenberg ; illustrated by Lynn Munsinger. -- 1st ed.
p. cm.
Summary: Having moved from the city to a tropical island to escape such horrifying creatures as bugs and cats, a homeowner encounters a horde of friendly crocodiles, who drink Tabasco sauce, get tangled in dental floss, and turn the house into a swamp.
ISBN-13: 978-0-316-07306-6
ISBN-10: 0-316-07306-7
[1. Crocodiles--Fiction. 2. Humorous stories. 3. Stories in rhyme.]
I. Munsinger, Lynn, ill. II. Title.
PZ8.3.G755Cro 2008
[E]--dc22

2006020571

10 9 8 7 6 5 4 3 2 1

CPI

Printed in China

It really is a pity
That you had to leave the city
Because of all the horrifying critters

GIANT tabby cats
And defiant scabby rats
Large enough to swallow baby-sitter

Roaches in your omelets
Pigeons dropping bomblets
Wild poodles stalking you in gangs

Squirrels in the trees
With LOTS and **LOTS** of fleas
And every single flea has tiny fangs

So you've traveled to an island
Tropical like Thailand
And left the grubby city you deplore

There are birds and butterfly
Breezes flutter by
Finally you are totally secure

Pudgy as a panda
Relaxed on your veranda
Wiggling your toes within your socks

You sadly have no notion
All around you, in the ocean
Are tons and tons of terrifying **CROCS**!

The day is dank and glum
The mailman hasn't come
The monkeys in the trees seem somewhat *nervous*

Your dog is strangely missing
Your kitty's started hissing
Your telephone has disconnected service

You're terribly annoyed
Very PARANOID
You race around your home to check the locks

Safe! You've checked them all
You're padding down the hall
And are smothered by a tidal wave of **CROCS!**

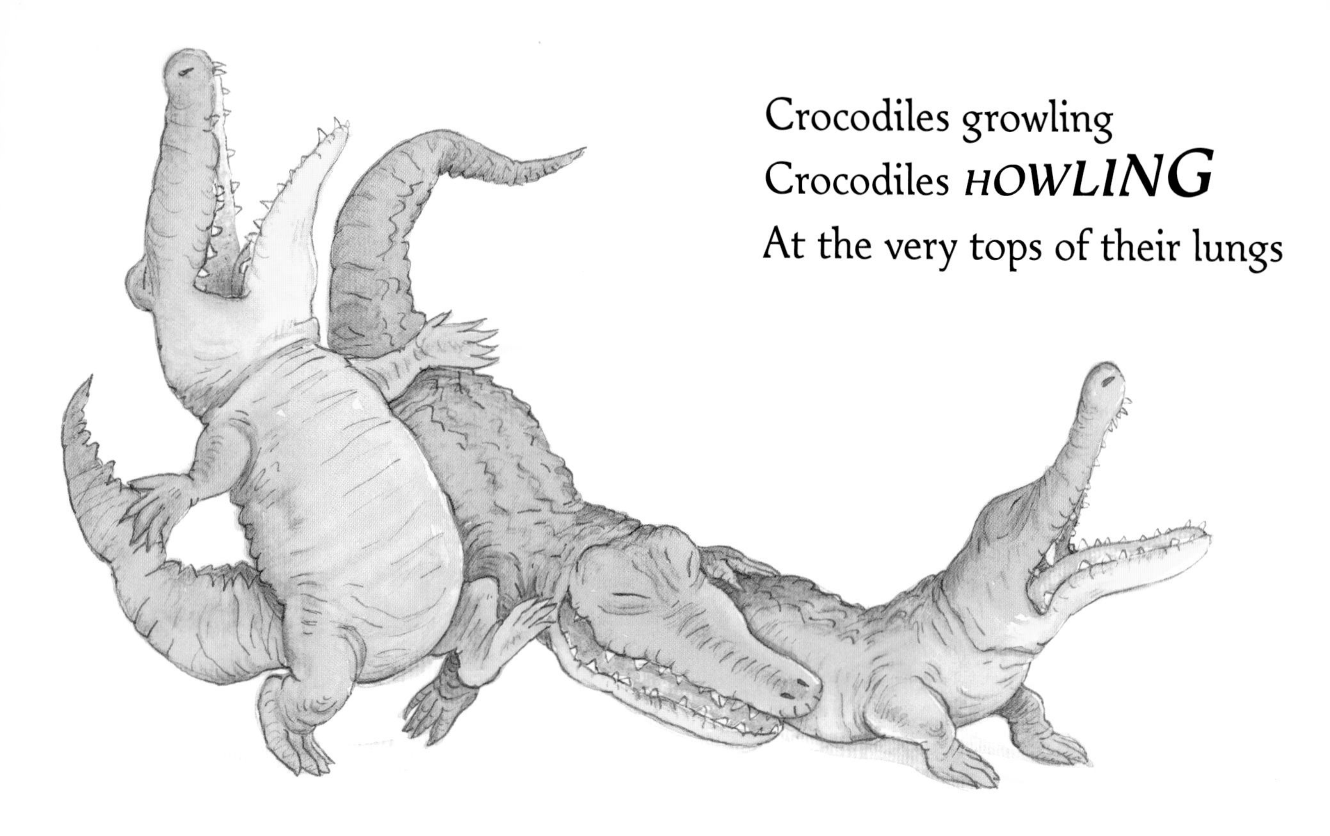

Crocodiles growling
Crocodiles *HOWLING*
At the very tops of their lungs

Crocodiles thrashing
Wildly smashing
Crocs with studs in their tongues

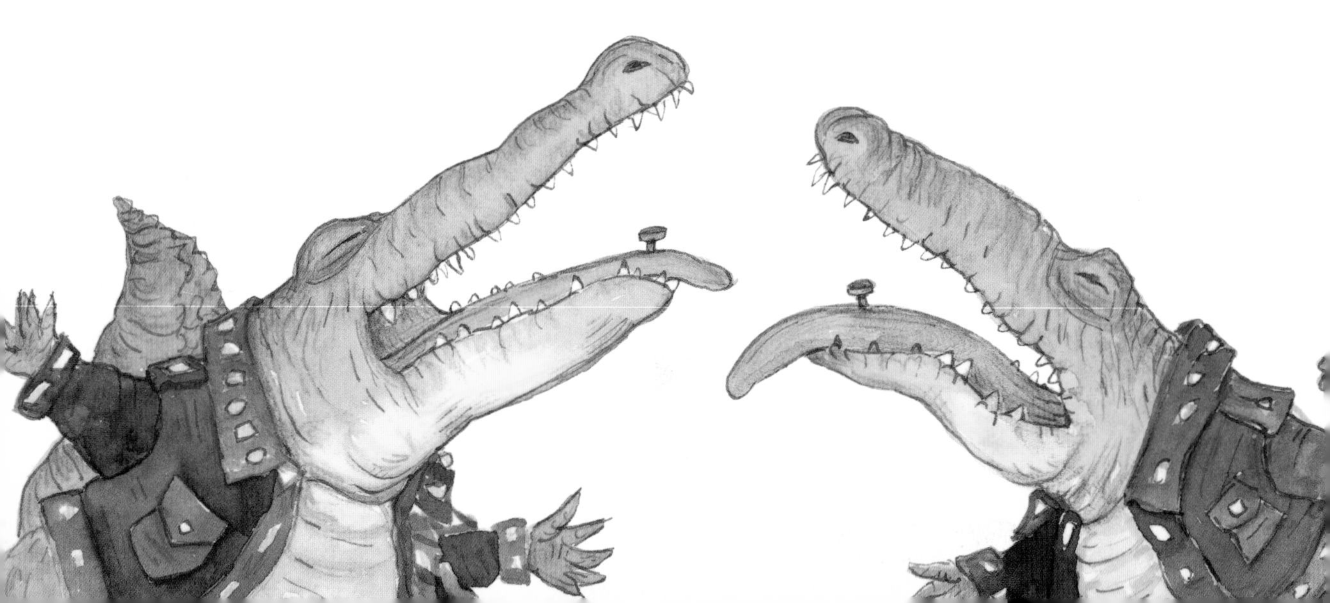

Crocs in disguises
Crocs of **all** sizes
Biting the knobs off of doors

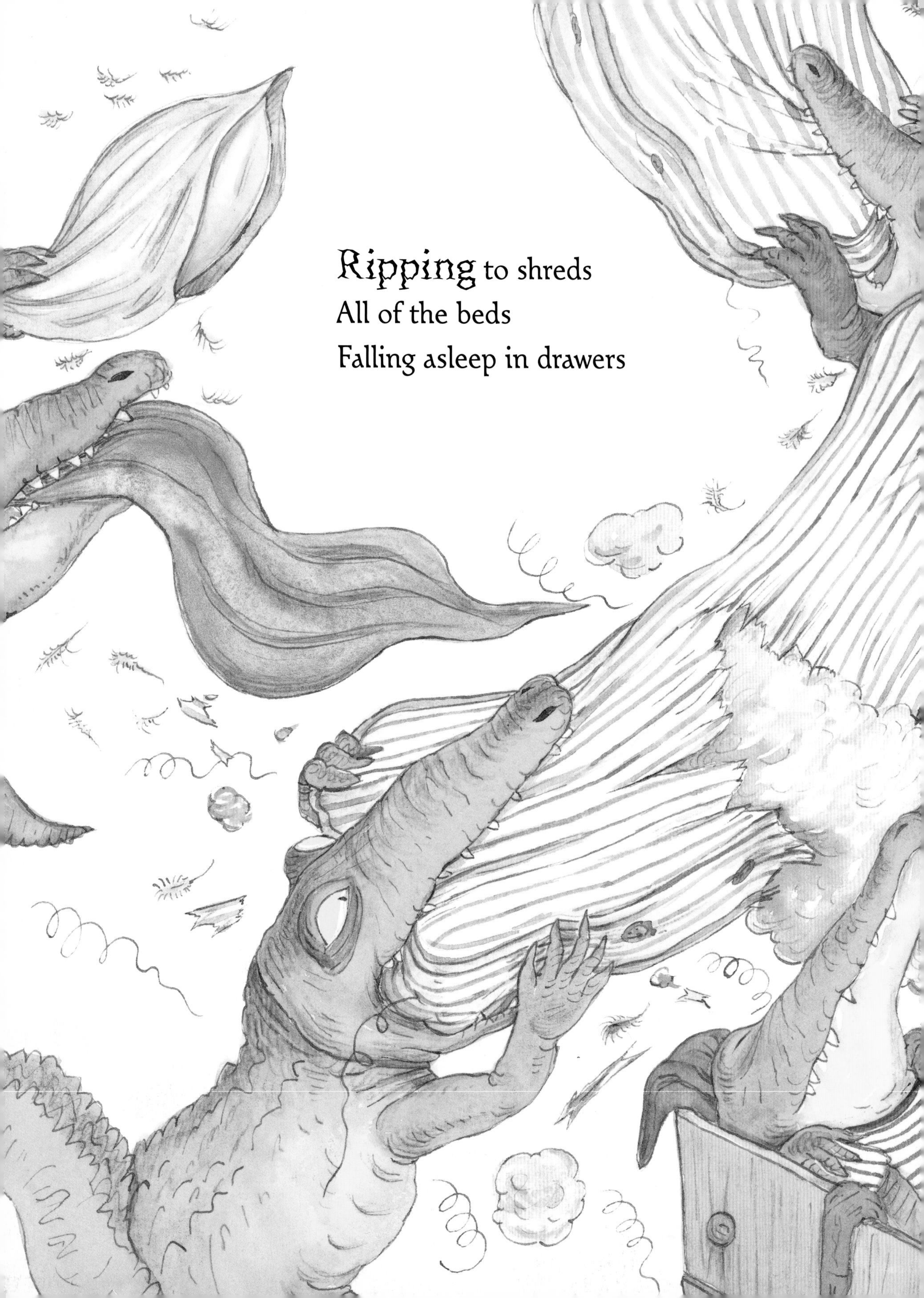

Ripping to shreds
All of the beds
Falling asleep in drawers

You're completely surrounded
Shocked and astounded
Collapsed on a pile of rugs

When all the crocs pause
Open their jaws
And **BOMBARD** you with kisses and hugs

Oh, they're wild when riled,
But, usually mild
Milder than a mouse

And they want to assure you
They *love* you, ***adore*** you!
Which is why they've moved into your house

So walk a croc
Around the block
Watch the neighbors flock and gawk

See oodles and oodles
Of crocs slurping noodles
A crocodile chef with a wok

Crocodile teens
In sagging jeans
Crocodile fireman, crocodile cop

Gobbling cake up
Putting on makeup
Painting their nails and going to shop

Crocs in your cupboard
Incredibly blubbered
Drinking Tabasco sauce

Pitiful SQUAWKS
From several crocs
Tangled in dental floss

Your home's now flooded
You've grown cold-blooded
You feel an instinctual urge

To scootch on your belly
Eat anything smelly
To slide into puddles, submerge

Your sleeping cubby
Is amazingly grubby
Made from buzzard boogers, dried

You're green like broccoli
Entirely croccoli
You're utterly satisfied

Then early one morning
Without any warning
There's a sickening seismic shock

It boggles your brain
But it's suddenly plain
Your island *itself* is a **CROC**!

You hold on tight
As he stands upright
And snaps at a lightning flash

Exhaling a spire
Of poisonous fire
He falls back in the sea with a CRASH

He swivels his eyes
Of mountainous size
And watches you stagger and stumble

He crashes his tail
Swallows a whale
Then speaks in a monstrous rumb

"At last I've awoken
So heed what I've spoken
I appoint you king of our nation

Rule fairly and sweetly
Or I'll eat you completely!"
He returns to deep hibernation

All the crocs sing
You're their crocodile king!
There's dancing, feasting, laughter

You're placed on a throne
(Your dog returns home!)
And you live snappily ever after